This book belongs to

....

make believe ideas ltd

The Wilderness, Berkhamsted, Hertfordshire, HP4 2AZ, UK.

www.makebelieveideas.com

Original poem by Clement Clarke Moore.
Illustrated by Clare Fennell.

'Twas the Night Before Christmas

Clement Clarke Moore

•

Clare Fennell

make
believe
ideas

'Twas the night before Christmas, when all through the house
not a creature was stirring, not even a mouse.
The stockings were hung by the chimney with care,
in hopes that St. Nicholas soon would be there.

The children were nestled all **snug** in their beds,
while visions of **sugarplums** danced in their heads.

And **Mamma** in her 'kerchief, and I in my cap,
had just settled down for a **long winter's** nap.

When out on the lawn there arose such a clatter,

I sprang from the bed to see what was the matter.

Away to the window

I flew like a flash,

tore open

the shutters and

threw up

the sash.

The moon, on the breast of the new-fallen snow,
gave the lustre of mid-day to objects below.

When, what to my wondering
eyes should appear . . .

. . . but a miniature sleigh and eight tiny reindeer,

with a little old driver, so lively and quick,

I knew in a moment it must be St. Nick.

More rapid than eagles his coursers they came,

and he whistled, and shouted,

and called them by name.

'Now, Dasher! Now, Dancer!

Now, Prancer and Vixen!

On, Comet! On, Cupid! On, Donner and Blitzen!

To the top of the porch! To the top of the wall!
Now, dash away! Dash away! Dash away all!"

As dry leaves that before the wild hurricane fly,

when met with an obstacle, mount to the sky;

so up to the housetop the coursers they flew,

with the sleigh full of toys, and St. Nicholas too.

And then, in a twinkling, I heard on the roof
the prancing and pawing of each little hoof.

As I **drew** in my head, and was turning around,
down the chimney St. Nicholas came with a **bound**.

He was dressed all in *fur*,
from his **head** to his **foot**,
and his clothes were all **tarnished**
with **ashes** and *soot*.

A bundle of *toys*
was **flung** on his back,
and he looked like a **peddler**
just *opening* his pack.

His eyes – how they *twinkled!* His dimples – how **merry!**
His **cheeks** were like *roses*, his nose like a **cherry!**
His **droll** little mouth was drawn up like a *bow*,
and the **beard** on his chin was as white as the *snow*.
The **stump** of a pipe he held **tight** in his teeth,
and the *smoke*, it encircled his head like a **wreath**.

He had a broad face and a little round belly
that shook when he laughed, like a bowlful of jelly!
He was chubby and plump, a right jolly old elf,
and I laughed when I saw him, in spite of myself.

A **wink** of his eye and a **twist** of his head

soon gave me to know I had **nothing** to dread.

He spoke **not** a word,

but went **straight** to his work,

and **filled** all the *stockings*;

then turned

with a **jerk**,

and laying his finger

aside of his nose,

and giving a nod,

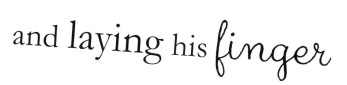

up the
chimney
he rose!

He sprang to his *sleigh*, to his **team** gave a *whistle*,
and away they all **flew**, like the down of a **thistle**.

But I heard him **exclaim**, as he drove out of sight,

"Happy Christmas to all,

and to **all** a *good night!*"